Alan Southall

The Charmed
Fascinatus

authorHOUSE®

AuthorHouse™ UK
1663 Liberty Drive
Bloomington, IN 47403 USA
www.authorhouse.co.uk
Phone: 0800.197.4150

Published by AuthorHouse 10/01/2018

ISBN: 978-1-5462-8738-4 (sc)
ISBN: 978-1-5462-8739-1 (hc)
ISBN: 978-1-5462-8737-7 (e)

Print information available on the last page.

Any people depicted in stock imagery provided by Thinkstock are models, and such images are being used for illustrative purposes only. Certain stock imagery © Thinkstock.

This book is printed on acid-free paper.

ACKNOWLEDGEMENTS

Many thanks for the team at the Apple Store in Liverpool for their kind assistance in helping to format this work and guidance in setting out the pages, for I have very little knowledge in this type of writing. I have only ever written long hand using a fountain pen prior to taking on this project.

The "Pages" AP has made the task more straight forward and I found it a very useful tool to write the manuscript.

Whilst I am studying Italian, I have very little memory of my grammar school lessons in Latin. Therefore, I wish to acknowledge the kind assistance of Steve Andrews, my Italian tutor in arranging the chapter translations.

I am grateful to my family members, especially my brothers David and Brian also Pete for their continued encouragement in tackling these pages.

This is a very short book and I wanted the manuscript put into a professional format mainly for my family and friends. I enjoy writing and have many journals, scribed over many years. So I wish to acknowledge the tremendous assistance of all those staff who assisted at AuthorHouse.

CONTENTS

105 AD, The Goldsmith was tasked with making a bracelet for the wealthy Legatus Crassus, who was in command of the legion based at Deva. Emperor Trajan had appointed Crassus due to his reputation in previous battles and control of other outposts in the empire. Castra Deva was now the home of the 20th legion and this encampment was considered one of the most strategic outposts of the empire. Having a harbour, the Roodee, lead and copper, excavated from the mines in the area, were distributed to many parts of the Empire. Trajan was completely satisfied that Crassus was the ideal person for this key position of Legatus, in total control.

The Legatus wanted the bracelet as a gift for his wife and requested that every effort should be made to make this charm unique and enchanting. It was to be the very best that the jeweller had made. Whilst Crassus was extremely wealthy and outwardly appeared a reasonable person, he lacked integrity and had many flaws in his manner. He was a cheat and a liar. This was not known by many, in fact only two in his command, a tribune and a centurion, based at Londinium, who had accompanied him on many battles which were fought and won over the years prior to the Deva posting. There was to be a third person to realise the flaws in his character, the goldsmith. For when advised that the bracelet was nearing completion and that payment was due in a short while, Crassus told the skilled jeweller that he would pay him only half its cost. Furthermore, he was advised not to complain for fear of him being sent into the Algerian mines for the remainder of his days. The bracelet had taken up most of the jeweller's time and he was extremely upset of this outcome. He would be hard pressed to pay all his costs and he and his family would now suffer for many many months. Thus threatened, the maker determined a strategy which would hopefully affect his piece of beauty and would cause the Legatus very much grief and make him suffer. Several weeks later, Afzal handed over the bracelet and told the recipient that the item was indeed extremely special and had a certain charm written in its design which was unique and unlike any other made by any other craftsmen, probably anywhere in the empire.[1]

2005 AD, The middle-aged couple, two people who recently met on a dating site, were having a day in Chester. They had gone there several times and enjoyed meeting up with new acquaintances at an art shop and cafe in the city. Their habit was to go first to the art shop for a look about, both being fond of art, then stroll down to the cafe which was near the river side. An Arab, called Afzal, owned the cafe and he also assisted any immigrants to settle in the area, in an official capacity as Middle East contact.

On this occasion, the couple were first heading towards a jeweller to browse rings. They noticed some loud noises as they approached the shop and then saw large excavators at work in the roadway as they approached the area. The man noticed something shining brightly on the pavement. It was a remarkable looking bracelet and when he picked it up it was very heavy. So much so, that he mentioned to his partner that it must be made of solid gold. This find was so appropriate as the couple were intending to select an engagement ring. They immediately thought that there might be some value to their find which could contribute towards the cost of the ring. Coincidence perhaps, but the bracelet had lain just outside the Milton pawn shop, next to the Grosvenor Hotel. They had spent several happy hours in the Grosvenor, enjoying morning teas.

Seconds later, both agreed to take the bracelet into the jewellers for valuation. They had no thought that the previous owner might be looking for the charm. Certainly, no one had approached them in this regard. The counter assistant asked if the item was for sale, his eyes totally fixed on the gold chain and the heavy links and special clasp. The

---

[1] Legion = 5240 Men, excluding officers, Includes 120 Cavalry
Legatus = Total Charge of a Legion
Tribune = 10 Per Legion
Centurion = In command of 100 men

clasp was curved, about half an inch long and covered in finely scribed wording, not English. The couple were keen to find out more about the item, however, the assistant didn't seem too knowledgeable and was unable to tell them any great detail. The lady being a little forceful requested if a manager was available to assist. Somewhat annoyed by this, the counter assistant called for Mr. Uruquart to come from his office.

The shop manager took out his eye piece and examined the bracelet very intently for about two minutes, a very long two minutes, murmuring as he did so. When challenged, the couple told him that it was an heir loom, left to the lady by her great aunt who was very wealthy. Uruquart coughed lightly, placed the bracelet carefully down onto a red handkerchief on the counter and made an immediate offer to buy it. It might have been that he was feeling particularly generous or had momentarily lost his sense according to the assistant, as he offered seventeen thousand pounds for it. He said that as far as he could tell, it was made by extremely skilled hands and was the best sample he had ever seen. Probably dating back to about 105 AD and made not far from where they stood. Each link was formed with subtle differences and scribed with messages in Latin. The clasp was of such precision that he believed it to be too perfect. This also had minutely scribed words. What would be very interesting should be to translate all the inscriptions as surely, they might mean something intriguing.

The couple gulped, eyed each other and explained they were on route for a coffee and brunch, during which time they would consider the very good offer. On stepping outside the shop, a light snow began falling, somehow adding a certain charm to the present situation. It was late Februarium and it seemed cold prior to entering the shop. The noise of the excavators faded in their minds as they were now aglow with their charm and the information the kindly Mr. Uruquart had provided, especially the value. They stopped simultaneously, gazed into one another's eyes and down onto the bracelet which was held by the gentlemen in a red handkerchief. Not the same red one that was used on the shop counter. "Oh, I have not seen you with a red one before, when did you get it?" his partner jested. For it seemed peculiar to have such a colour. She had not noticed the three initials sewn neatly in one corner. His immediate response was to suggest that his fiancé to be, should wear the bracelet on their way down to Afzal's. "You might get to like it and for sure, it looks exceptional on your wrist. I am certain, when we order our usual scrambled eggs with smoked salmon, you might just flash it past Afzal for his comment". Unknown to the couple, the Syrian, in addition to owning the neat little Bistro and being the official responsible for settling in any Syrian immigrants into the North West, had a family tree which went back many generations even back to Roman times and beyond. All the families had been involved in jewellery since founding their business of making exotic jewellery in Rome, having moved from Syria. The happy couple, now enjoying their brunch had not even the slightest knowledge of the history associated with their find on that pavement. The bracelet hung heavy on Janes' wrist. Mike thought that somehow though, her appearance was improved and gave a certain sparkle in her eyes. In all, Jane was very pleased to have on her person the most exotic piece ever to arrive back in Chester after some time. Afzal came into the café and, as usual when he saw them, he made his way over to Mike and Jane to great them. He looked a little jaded but perked up as he sat down in anticipation of having the enjoyable banter which was the norm when all three got together. Mike began to relate the tale of their find outside the jewellers in the city centre. Afzal glanced over to Jane and saw the bracelet. He immediately began to heavily perspire. He rubbed his eyes over and over until a rash started to appear over his forehead. He beckoned a waitress to urgently bring him a glass of water. He told the couple that he was having a particularly difficult time with the family recently arrived in the UK who insisted in living in an area called Heswall on the Wirral. He has tried to explain that this area was rather exclusive with many millionaires living there. In fact, more wealthy families in that area than all of Merseyside. Whilst the Syrian family were wealthy, Afzal was finding it rather hard to find a property and how they could readily assimilate in that area. This problem, whilst causing Afzal a headache, paled into insignificance as he continually gazed upon the golden charm wrapped around Janes wrist. He went over the many years recalling his father's tale of a Roman bracelet. A bracelet specially made in Deva for the head of the twentieth legion stationed there. His tale was very detailed, so much so, that Afzal had drawn a picture of the charm in his mind and now it became reality. The link with the Afzal family was magical and created strong images of what transpired all those centuries ago. The story deserved telling and probably worthy of a short book. The fifteen links and the clasp, each with its inscriptions.[2]

Thus the story begins; we move back 1900 years, we will return to Chester later.

---

[2] Some 1900 tears prior, a highly skilled Goldsmith had punched a message on the clasp. This message together with the writings on the links had been difficult to decipher.

FIRST CHAIN LINK

DOMINA FATUM ATTRAHIT

The Lady Attracts Fatality

1 05 AD, On the day Crassus and his wife were given their bracelet, they were so happy. They gazed in amazement at its beauty and Lucretia thanked the jeweller for all his skilled work. The jeweller, although cheated in his endeavours, appeared somewhat at ease and had a smile of contentment. He did not accept the hand shake from Crassus but did not make any adverse comments to him for fear of what may be done if the Legatus was upset at all. Having taken possession of the charm at the Jewellers shop, and having spent an hour enjoying some wine at the shop, the happy couple returned to their splendid villa in the suburbs of Deva, However, on entering the living area, two things happened. First, Lucretia looked down at her wrist, the bracelet had gone. Second, a note from the Emperor Trajan saying that they must immediately depart for Rome. The baggage carriages were in position, with horses at the ready, their belongings packed and a suitable guard to protect them on their long journey. No time to retrace their steps to find the bracelet.

Crassus quickly scribed a note and map to his best friend Drakis, to follow a certain route as soon as possible to find the treasure. He gave the note to one of his many servants to pass on very speedily with an incentive, a gold denarius. The couple were devastated, especially the lady. She had come to be entranced by its beauty and was keen to start trying to decipher the minute wording on each link. Even after wearing it for such a short time, it had somehow made her feel and look relaxed and more attractive. Lucretia was so sad to lose it that she became deeply depressed. Although he tried to reassure and console her with promises that Drakis would recover the treasure, Crassus, deep down felt it lost forever. Such was the grief in the lady, that she became extremely ill over the passing days. So much so, and probably also due to the horrendous journey across the territories towards Rome, that she finally and suddenly gave out. Lucretia passed away. The cause of her demise confused and troubled all who had seen her. Her appearance changed quite dramatically following the loss of the charm. It was as though she had, within hours, aged about ten years. The demented Crassus continued his journey and his fate was sealed. He became one of Rome's most revered leaders. He did not however manage to find another partner and he died a recluse on the Island Sardinia across the Tyrrleneum sea. He was found out as a cheat and liar and tried to even fool Emperor Trajan, which was his final undoing.

SECOND CHAIN LINK

NEX MENTI SAEPE IMPERAY

◆◆◆

Murder Often Controls the Mind

Within ten minutes of Drakis receiving the note, handed to him by the servant, he had gathered twelve trustworthy colleagues, and took to the map. Following the route given, they spread across the roads in search of the bracelet. One of the party was keener than the others. Lupus, or the wolf, as he was known, was recognised by the loss of his left arm in battle. Whilst the legion retained him as a discens, or private, he had very little chance of any promotion. His earnings therefore would be very restricted. His father had deserted the family when the four siblings where quite young and Lupus' mother had struggled to keep food on the table. Being the oldest, Lupus was always keen to bring some relief to the family. Finding the charm would surely bring him some rewards. His mind was active and he also quickly considered that if he was to find and keep the bracelet, then this may provide the means for him to take his family away from the slum area where they lived. They would start a new life elsewhere. He determined that he would not give up the bracelet to Drakis if he were to find it.

Lupus pulled away from the others, who were conducting an arm linked search along the paths and roads which the couple had taken to their villa. He explained to Drakis that he had promised to assist his poor Mother in some home repairs and had forgotten these chores when agreeing to join the group. When Drakis had called the group together, Lupus had seen that the start point on the map was Afzal's Jewellery shop. Lupus immediately made for Afzal's place. On arrival, the assistant explained that Afzal had gone to see a customer to take instruction for a necklace. Lupus asked where Crassus had been seated earlier when taking the special jewel. He did not need to describe the Legatus fully, only just mentioning his purple tunic with gold depiction of a trimarine was sufficient. A small finger pointed in the direction of a corner seat which had several plush cushions which were embroidered with images of Rome. Lupus gave a very discreet smile as a sharp glint emanating from beneath one of these cushions, caught his eye. Not wanting to attract undue attention, Lupus beckoned the young girl to fetch him a small cup of red wine as he made his way to the corner seat. When the girl had gone and when he had made certain no one was looking in his direction, Lupus placed a small red cloth from his tunic pocket, over the bracelet and drew it into his inside chest pocket.

Task accomplished in all ways, Lupus decided he should finish his wine, then casually leave and return to his family, some thirty minutes' walk away. He must not rush as this might attract attention. He was just taking his final sip of the delicious wine, when Afzal strode in. If ever a man looked troubled it was him. He was reflecting on all his financial problems. There was insignificant money to purchase new materials for future orders and his task to persuade new clients to take old designs worried him. He had lost his latest prospect. His hatred of Crassus was taking its toll. His only glimmer of hope was that his secret inscription would take effect and avenge his treatment by the head of the twentieth legion. Afzal made his way to where Lupus sat and mumbled some words. Amongst these was mention of a golden bracelet. Thus, Lupus was urged to ask the man opposite what he meant about the bracelet. He realised too late, that indeed there was a story to be told and he became transfixed as Afzal related the story of his contract with Crassus and how he had been wronged. So much money lost that it would cause the jeweller many years of hardship and, if ever, he could return to his previous status as master jeweller of the Empire, Afzal said that the finished bracelet had considered all this misery and the evil action and threats by Crassus. He did not want to embellish his story any further.

It was probably thirty minutes that Lupus had been in the shop and he was pleased to finally say his goodbyes and leave for home. Immediately on leaving, he noticed Drakis and the others making for the shop, he quickly entered an alleyway and later met his family. His Mother could hardly hold back her tears of joy when she heard the plan. They would head South for Londinium from where they would consider going further by ship to the continent, following sale of the charm. Maria, Lupus' mother requested to wear the bracelet on route, it certainly improved her appearance. She had not been very well of late and with the trauma of all the prior years of hardship, the much-needed lift was very much due. The carriage which Lupus had acquired was very basic, only one horse and only just room for the family members, and minimum of belongings to support their journey.

Lupus' next younger brother, Video, was, by nature, extremely alert. He did not need to be told the value of the charm. He took an immediate shine to the bracelet and his mind became damaged with his desire to have it for himself. By the time the party had reached Lactodorum[3] he had seen enough. Why should he share the wealth with his mother and siblings? He had become entranced and his thoughts showed a bright future for himself but not for his mother. The eve of the second day of leaving the town, his mother collapsed in agony clutching her stomach. The bracelet lay a short distance from where Maria lay, stricken by a mystery illness, and where she had fallen heavily on the floor. Video had been first to the scene and immediately took hold of the charm placing it under his shirt. He screamed for help and his brothers arrived, headed by Lupus. They could hardly hold their grief as Maria slowly but surely slipped away into the heavens above. They noticed her appearance had changed and she no longer had a sense of happiness. It took only a second for them to realise that the bracelet was not on her wrist. They immediately challenged Video as he was clearly on the scene prior to their arrival. Video showed no sign of guilt and suggested that Maria had been attacked by thieves for the bracelet, surely it was a mistake for her to wear this in Lactodorum, a place not familiar to them? By this time Video had been taken over by the charm and his manner strengthened on any accusations. Lupus now felt that he should tell the tale of what he knew of the bracelet and its origins. He related the terrible tale of treachery and misery surrounding the charm, so all believed it was 'good riddance' to it. All acts had a purpose and with their Mother now gone, the brothers agreed to proceed with the plan to go to Londinium. Fate had spoken and taken a hand in the disappearance of the bracelet, and

---

[3] Lactodorum = Towcester

possibly now bring some good fortune with it gone. That evening, a prayer and sacrifice was offered to SPES.

The following morning only three brothers sat at the table. The remaining brothers then made a further decision not to continue South. Lupus was told by a Monachus in the town of good prospects of work in Mona. He persuaded the others that their fortune may well live in this place.[4]

---

[4] Discens = Private Soldiers in Roman Army
Trimarine = Roman Warship
Londinium = London in Roman Times
SPES = Roman Goddess of Hope
Monachus = Monk

THIRD CHAIN LINK

ET RISUM ET CALAMITATEM EFFICERE POTE ST FILIA PULCHRA

<hr>

A Beautiful Daughter Can Cause Laughter and Tragedy

Video did not wear the bracelet, he placed it into his leather pouch, worn around his waist. The fact that the gold did not embrace his skin, did not deter the missions embedded in the minute inscriptions on the chain links. It was as if time was held in abeyance, for surely, it would not be long before a wrist became available? It was essential for actions to continue in order that the final clasp was to be reached. The promises required fulfilment.

How odd, thought video, the all-seeing, that he had visions of his three brothers finding contentment away from Londinium. Also, he began to sweat profusely at each step he took going South. He had a repeat vision of finding an Inn on his route, where he would meet a beautiful young girl. Was the charm making him deluded? On the second day after leaving his brothers, he came across an Inn and was greeted by an enchanting and beautiful young lady. His vision became reality. He felt a strong urge to pursue his dream and a certain strength to succeed, which seemed to come from the golden charm in his pouch. It happened at tre horae in the morning. He woke the maiden and to impress her to accept him he dared to show her the bracelet, which he fixed around her wrist as she gave herself to him. Carmen was impressed and following the binding of the bracelet and their bodies, they lay together and slept until dawn. Rosy fingered dawn awoke Video and he gazed down at his prize. He saw that she was partly dressed and this troubled him as he felt certain that Carmen had not moved from his side when they laid naked together. However, even worse, the bracelet was no longer on her wrist. He tried to wake her to ask what had happened. Carmen did not stir at all and after being checked by others at the Inn, she was declared unfortunately gone to a better place. Video could not hold his sadness, even though it was a short time, he had had happy hours with the Innkeepers daughter. He saw no reason to stay and started again South. Along a dirt track through a wooden area, the Innkeeper struck a blow to the back of Video's head and Video joined his mother. Dragging the body into the undergrowth, the Innkeeper noticed a leather pouch around Video's body. He unclasped this and shaking out the contents, slipped the pouch into his saddle.

Two days following, a lady of leisure, a meretrix was walking along this track on her way North. She was on her way to meet her master in Deva. The very wealthy and handsome Crassus. As she ambled lazily along the path thinking of the wonderful times she would be sharing with her lover, she noticed a red cloth laying in the grass. As she stooped to examine her find, she immediately jumped back in surprise. Under the cloth, lay a most beautiful golden bracelet.

FOURTH CHAIN LINK

EDACITUS DOLOREM EFFICELE POTEST SEMPITEMUM

◇◈◇

Greed Can Cause Everything Pain

2005, Mike and Jane couldn't wait to be on their own again to decide what to do next. Should they keep the item or sell it to Milton's for an immediate £17,000.00? Mike was not a very intelligent chap but he realised that if Mr Uruquart was offering such a large amount on sight of the item, then it might be worth much more than this. In fact, he became filled with greed and convinced himself and Jane that it could be worth at least double that amount. He suggested they go straight home and explore the internet. Afzal's tale made him think it might be a very famous lost jewel. Jane reluctantly agreed, she was still wanting to browse the engagement rings. Wearing the bracelet, had made some changes to Jane's appearance. As they walked along, she felt as though her looks had improved, her eyes began to sparkle and even Mike smiled more as he looked at her. Mike was somewhat disturbed about Afzal's story and reaction. Was he trying to attempt prior ownership? As they made their way along, Jane remembered the red handkerchief, but did not raise the subject. The couple were making their way back to the area where the Park and Ride bus stopped. They decided not to go along their normal route past Milton's or the Grosvenor and Mike suggested keeping clear of any main roads. One of the paths was much narrower than the others and Mike seemed very familiar with it. Half way down and on the left, was an emblem etched into a stone which shocked Jane. It was in the form of a man's privates fully erect with all accoutrements. She saw a slight smile in Mikes face. She then noticed a plaque nearby explaining that in Roman times this was a symbol used to depict a brothel. What she failed to see was a smaller plaque, some feet above this, advertising the modern version. This was two doors further back along the alley, for you could not call this a roadway, too narrow for a car. This brothel was open twenty-four seven and a notice board beside the door explained that every client would be given a red handkerchief with the initial C when first joining the club. If also desired, the initials of their favourite girl could be added for the generous sum of one hundred pound. This would help to guarantee her being with the client when next available. Unaware of this detail, Jane continued to follow Mike towards the bus depot. She held his hand firmly, not for fear of losing him as he strode along quickly, but due to her anger, she felt that Mike was not being totally honest when she challenged him regarding whether he had been in that alley way before. He relentlessly denied even knowing the place existed. It was not long before the couple reached the bus station. Jane was amazed that they managed to find it, so many turns, alleys, crossing so many roads and even ascending and descending the rows at times. Jane was totally exhausted as they took their places in the queue just as the Park and Ride bus pulled in. The couple held each other close and suddenly Jane let out a fierce scream, startling the others queuing. Mike was stunned and momentarily speechless. The bracelet had gone from Janes wrist. He immediately grasped Janes hand and burst through the gathering crowd shouting that they must retrace their steps. Jane continued to exclaim "how, we will never be able to do that?". Mike suggested that at least the route was out of the way and not many may have gone along those paths. After only a few minutes the couple were completely convinced that they had not retraced their steps correctly. [perhaps 2005 was turning out to be a year of disappointment for the couple, even more as they were to discover within a very short time.] A peculiar looking middle-aged gentleman in a trilby and long overcoat came towards them. Mike noticed a red handkerchief protruding from his top coat pocket, and went towards him, pulling the chap to one side. He quietly asked him for directions to the 'C' club. The way led them along an extremely narrow alley that Mike did not recall. Mike had by now gone a short way in front of Jane. A loud crash was heard from above. Mike speeded up urging Jane to quickly follow him. Too late. The large wooden sign advertising the 'Taberna Vostra', which had hung for more than one hundred and fifty years, came crashing like a lead weight onto Jane's cranium, killing her outright.[5]

---

[5] Rows = Elevated Shopping Area

The charm's prophecy had come to life again after so many years lying dormant. It would be active for a further 15 years and hold many of its admirers in its power without them ever realising the spell.

FIFTH CHAIN LINK

POTUS IMMODICUS IN PERICULUM ARCESSIT

—◆◈◆—

Excess drinking creates danger

As he walked in, or more likely waltzed in, anyone could sense the absolute pleasure in this gentleman's manner. He threw his trilby accurately onto the hat stand with such ease that it was obvious he had done this many times before. He took more care in doffing his overcoat. For within its velveted inside pocket was stored a beautiful bracelet. He took out his red handkerchief, placed it onto the large oak table and placed the charm onto it. He locked the door and began to contemplate his next moves. Charles was the youngest of eight children born into the Dalgleish family. They who owned three hundred acres, the Belmont Estate in Cheshire. He had behaved very badly the year before and was urged to go abroad for a long holiday. He had spent twelve months in France and it was his only Sister's birthday which caused his return. He was allowed back to attend the special party and then for only three days. The party had been the day before, as in effect Charles had only a short period before leaving. That morning, he decided to visit, once more, his favourite venue for entertainment. He was unable to resist the lure of the beautiful girls who worked in the Chester house. He felt they were more attractive than any of those he had seen in the many brothels in France he had frequented.

He had got into serious difficulties on his prior visit a year ago, before being expelled due to his stupidity. He had primed a young lady to return to the mansion with him after their session at the "C". Unknown to him, the young lady he had lain with and desired for more, had not long been released from Risely Women's prison for theft. Not just a simple act of thieving from a shop, but theft of precious gems worth many thousands of pounds from a jeweller in Chester city centre. She had two accomplices and the two were armed with handguns, threatening the staff just after closing. She was caught through her greed to convert some jewellery for cash in a pub in Liverpool. Unfortunately for her, a plain clothed police man was in there for some lunch, a pie and a pint. The item was a Cup Winners Cup medal and all stations had been alerted.

Unaware of this history, Charles was so pleased that Constance had accepted his invitation, for the right price, to spend more time with him. She was very pretty and he was looking forward to the promised hour of pleasure. After slipping a small potion into his drink, she began collecting several items from the glass cabinet, putting them into her large handbag. Charles was using his Sisters room for his dalliance, knowing that she was away on business in Manchester for several days. In his now dazed and helpless state, Charles could not foretell that Constance had managed to take items to the value of one hundred and sixty thousand pound and she was able to convert these to cash very quickly. When he awoke from his stupor, Charles had no time to gather his thoughts as two of the servants had come into the room hearing noises. They knew Vivienne was away and became suspicious at the sounds of breaking glass, so Charles had no option but to disclose his actions to the family. He could not blame the theft on intruders. Being upright and honest people, the family did not want their name tarnished with reports that the youngest son had associations with a brothel and even invited a prostitute into their home. Therefore, they did not call the police nor did they make a claim on insurance. Vivienne was most upset as a special ring given to her by her grandmother, was one of the items taken. Neither Vivienne nor any of the other family members would forgive Charles and he was banished for twelve months.

So here now was Charles gazing at what appeared to him, to be a very precious item, the most exquisite he had seen. He scribbled a brief note to the family, expressing his thanks for allowing him back for the party. He said also, that he hoped he would be invited again next year.

Twelve hours later Charles met his girlfriend Michelle at her bungalow in Pontoise, North of Paris. She was very pleased to see him, more so when he showed her the new present he had brought back with him. Michelle was so pleased with his attention that she gave herself to him, not long after opening the door. As they lay exhausted on the floor in the hallway, she slipped the bracelet onto her wrist without Charles realising. Within thirty minutes the lovers had packed some essentials into one case and were heading South to Paris. The weather had changed for the worse, but this did not deter them, they had promised themselves this treat when next they met up. They were on the motorway heading for Michelle's father's boat which was moored along the Seine. They had planned to spend some time enjoying themselves in absolute luxury. Now they had a bonus to keep themselves happier. The boat had two crew and that was ideal, Charles himself had become quite proficient in handling the craft following instruction from Michelle's Father. He relished the role of 'captain' and even more, wearing the cap of recognition, being quite vain. Prior to casting off, Michelle realised they were running low in alcohol and, in particular, champagne. She made her way to her favourite wine store a short distance away.

She returned in ten minutes, poured celebratory drinks as Charles and crew joined her, when disaster struck in several ways. A bright light hit the deck as a firework, from a party on shore, exploded causing severe flames, then a large jolt and sounds of crumbling metal. One of the river barges had ploughed into their boat. At this point, Charles noticed the bracelet was no longer on Michelle's wrist. He had no time to ask her where it might be as the last he saw of her was as she was flung over board in the collision. She had little chance of survival, she was quite inebriated and had hit her head on one of the stanchions holding the railings, as her body was jettisoned into the Seine. Her body was never recovered.

Charles was inconsolable. He launched a tirade of verbal abuse at the river barge and threw a boat spike towards one of it's crew. Within a few minutes, he realised that Michelle was lost and asking his crew to alert the authorities. He made his way ashore. He had remembered that he saw the charm on Michelle's wrist as she went ashore, so he determined that it may have been lost as she went to or from the wine store. He was heading there quickly.

VESTIMENTA ATRA FORSITAN NON SALVUM FACIANT

Wearing Black May Not Be Safe

At exactly the time as Michelle was being catapulted from the boat deck, the bracelet was spotted just outside the wine store by a passing soldier. His uniform showed that he was a member of an elite helicopter squadron, based in Nancy, a long way East of Paris. He had just finished two weeks leave which he had spent with his aged and wealthy Aunt. She owned a popular boutique in Paris near Montmartre. Emile was her favourite and she had openly declared that having no children of her own, all would be left to him in her will. Having stowed the bracelet into a secure pocket on his uniform, he made his way back to say goodbye to his Aunt. He did not tell her of his find and he decided that he would keep it as a surprise for his beautiful girlfriend. Emile had known her for only eight months. They met when Emile was stationed for an exchange tour at the Air Base at El Blida in Algeria. His squadron had carried out two years of surveillance in that area of desert, assisting in checking the progress of possible terrorists. The outlying villages were a target for extremists and quite often, Emile also carried out "on the ground" checks. It was during one of these searches that he met Renee at one of the local bars. It was love at first sight.

Her family pleaded with her not to leave and go back to France. However, it didn't take much persuading for Emile to describe all the benefits of living in the trappings of the area near Nancy, compared to the suburbs surrounding El Blida.

They clung to each other for at least five minutes. The two weeks had seemed like two months. It was the first time that Renee had been left on her own during a holiday period of Emile's. She could not understand Emile's reasoning. He had explained that it was very important for his Aunt to think that she was the most important person in his life due to the will. Had she known the Aunt, she would have very quickly understood the main reason. Renee was of African origin and while Emile treasured her jet-black skin, the Aunt would have been horrified. Maude was not even aware that Emile had a girlfriend, so taking her with him was impossible to consider.

Emile knew he had in his possession an extremely valuable piece. On arrival in Nancy, he had it valued by a reputable jeweller, explaining that it was a gift from his wealthy Aunt in Paris. That jeweller had offered two hundred and fifty thousand euros for it.

The golden bracelet looked even more valuable on Renee's shiny black wrist. Emile gazed at her beauty which seemed enhanced tenfold by wearing the jewel. She looked charming. Their provisions were running low, so Renee decided to go into the local market. She was going to cook a special meal that evening to celebrate. Celebrate something that Emile was yet to realise, she was pregnant. She donned her favourite black short sleeved dress and kissed Emile passionately as she left for the shopping. Now wearing all black and together with her beautiful black skin, the bracelet shone like a beacon. Emile had finally agreed for her to wear it, after much persuasion.

As she strolled along the cobbled streets, Renee pondered over the future. How lucky she was meeting, falling in love and now living with her handsome, now wealthy solider. The route to the market included walking along some narrow alley ways, but she had done this many times before. The difference that day, was the attraction caused by the brightly shining light on her wrist. As she passed a receded doorway, the knife struck her in the back, very deep and murderous.

Remus had been watching the unfortunate lady, drawn to her by the gleaming gold bracelet on her black shiny skin. As she fell, the bracelet loosened and fell beside her, lying on part of her black dress. The thief and murderer fled like a rabbit. He was well known by the authorities in Nancy and had been on parole to visit his Mother. He was serving ten years for aggravated burglary and had slipped his guard. Over the years, Remus had befriended a corrupt jeweller in Nancy and he headed immediately to him, stuffing the charm into his trouser pocket. He was sweating profusely when he met up with Pascal.

SEVENTH CHAIN LINK

IGNIS OMNIA MOTAT

———◆◆◆———

Fire Changes Everything

P ascal did not enquire how Remus had acquired the piece, he suspected he had done a great deal of mischief to be in possession. His anxious manner, played into the jeweller's hands. He slipped five thousand euros into Remus palm and bid him leave very quickly. Pascal then spent some time examining the bracelet. He noted that each chain link had minute Latin inscriptions and the clasp had even more microscopic writing. It was immaculate and he noted a date showing 105 AD. His instincts told him not to try to sell this in France, he would need to go overseas. The police in France would now be on full alert for any information relating to this extremely valuable golden charm. He determined to translate all the writings at some future date. He needed to move rapidly as he was certain Remus would be apprehended and reveal how he came to have so much cash in his possession.

Pascal had a Sister in Australia and he was planning to visit her in a few weeks. He had his VISA stamped into his passport so he just needed to sort his flights, pack, then go. There were several alternatives to choose from. He finally decided for a flight which included a stopover in Singapore. He had always wanted to visit this area and he felt that a break was ideal, otherwise the journey would be far too strenuous to complete in one twenty-four-hour spell. He booked a single to Singapore then a second flight to Sydney a few days later. He kept his treasure in a small pouch in his hand luggage so that it was always with him on the trip.

The heat on leaving the aircraft cabin and entering the gangway, nearly knocked him over. He had never travelled to the far East before and he was overcome by the temperature. Having settled into his room at a recently renovated hotel, he decided to explore some of the popular tourist spots recommended by his travel agents. His charm was secure in his safe in the room and he was confident that was the best place for it. As for the bracelet, this was not ideal for it did not appreciate being hidden away in a tiny metal box. Pascal was out for about six hours, spending time site seeing and enjoying a good meal at the Quan Hoe Soon suggested by a fellow guest at the hotel. What struck him, was how clean the streets were. Not a speck of rubbish and no chewing gum splattered on the paving. He learned that heavy fines were imposed on everyone seen dropping litter or throwing gum.

He felt the excess heat from the flames within two hundred metres from his hotel. Pascal panicked, he raced to the scene, in vain, to see his hotel reduced to rubble. The fire service was in the process of damping down the three-story Travel Inn style building where he was staying. He eagerly challenged the Chief of police, who was in attendance, to assist him finding the room safe. It was all in vain, he was told to keep clear and not go near the scene for at least another twenty-four hours. He lodged an official request for recovery of the safe from room eighteen and gave his mobile number and his sister's address in Sydney. Pascal could not see how anything could have survived the wreckage caused by the ferocious fire. In his heart, he felt the bracelet lost; with only a glimmer of hope in seeing it again, he resigned to proceeding on with his journey to Australia.

EIGHTH CHAIN LINK

VIRGAE METANICAE DESUPER OCCIDERE POSSUNT

<figure>❖❖❖</figure>

Metal Rods from Above Can Be Fatal

The stylish Singapore Airline's stewardess checked in to the London Hilton with other crew members. The flight to London Heathrow from Singapore had been pleasant enough apart from the usual turbulence over part of the Indian continent. Mintah was particularly beautiful and one or two of the first-class passengers had been a little too keen in their friendly approaches. She was experienced enough and handled the situation without causing too much embarrassment, Mintah was here on a mission. She checked into her room and examined the gold bracelet in her handbag. Her boyfriend, a fireman in the Singapore fire service, had passed it to her after finding it amongst the rubble of the hotel. He had little time to explain that, on arrival in London, she should seek out two well established jewellers and obtain quotations. She should then sell it, insisting on a cash transaction, returning a few days later on her next flight back to Singapore.

When naming their first-born son, the Indian couple chose Agni, the name being associated with sacred fire. So, it seemed destined that Agni would, one day, find his fortune associated with his name. He had left Delhi, seeking a new life further East and finally settled in Singapore. He was fortunate to gain employment in the fire service which, of course led him to his wealth. On finding the bracelet inside room safe number eighteen, he decided immediately, not to declare it. The box had protected the item inside and needed a sharp twist with his axe on the hinge, to open and reveal the treasure. Agni had always been an honest man, up to that moment when he viewed the golden charm. He was enthralled and within an hour, he had an estimated value of two hundred thousand US dollars made on it by an acquaintance. He told Mintah that she must not accept anything less.

The morning after her arrival in London, Mintah dressed, had a continental breakfast delivered to her room, put on the bracelet and left the hotel. The concierge had given her names of three creditable jewellers. She was not familiar with travelling around the city, so she decided the best and quickest way was by taxi. She began walking in the direction of the nearest jewellers, keeping an eye for a taxis and it was extremely busy. The pavements were crowded with many people trying to hail cabs and there were several phut phut type of vehicles. Mintah had seen these in films frequently shown during the flights in first class cabins. That means of transport was also common in the far East, especially Thailand and the Ape was the quickest means of transport around the busy, narrow roads in Capri. They were motorised three-wheel carriages, the motors being similar to low CC motorcycles. What she saw here in London as she desperately tried to get a cab, were three-wheel carriages but operated by a push bike arrangement. They seemed to be able to weave onto the pavements and even go in the opposite direction of traffic tempting customers to climb onboard. She was beginning to despair when one of these tricycles sped up to her and a voice called loudly for her to step up onto the rear seat. Simultaneously a black cab was doing a U turn, having spotted her and was aiming to secure his fare. At the precise moment the tricycle arrived at her side, the black cab had completed his manoeuvre. The altercation was a crowd pleaser and Mintah could not understand many of the phrases being used. It became physical when she was virtually pulled into the small carriage behind the trike and was on her way. The cyclist did his best to gather speed but it was no match for the black cab driver. On impact, she was flung out of the seat and onto the paving. The tricycle overturned and the black cab smashed into a corner upright of the scaffolding being erected over the shop nearby. Events over the short period were beyond comprehension.

Coming to her senses, Mintah noticed that the bracelet was no longer on her wrist. She heard a loud noise and a piece of scaffolding, followed by three heavy planks, came crashing down on her, killing her outright. The bracelet spun towards the shop doorway, being inhabited by one of London's many homeless unfortunates.

NINTH CHAIN LINK

A SORORIBUS PROMITTENTIBUS CAVETE

❖◆◆◆❖

Take Care When Sisters Make Promises

2014, Many years went by without incident. The main reason related to the poor gentlemen who sat in the doorway that fateful day. He was one of many hundreds who inhabit the streets of London and other cities across the UK. 'Old Bill' as he was known, had done his duty and finally disgarded by society. What made his situation worse, was that he was blind. He was a war veteran and his family knew little of his plight. In fact, his wife and two sisters had not seen him for many years. He kept a small piece of paper in a pocket, which had his wife's name, Frances and her address together with the address of his two siblings. 'Old Bill' had left his wife for a life of poverty in London, feeling that he would become a massive burden on her. Being blinded in action and on return from hospital, he was told that his wife was very poorly. Frances was suffering from uncontrollable fits and needing one hundred percent care. His decision was simple to him. He did not want to impose any additional suffering on her, which forced him, in his mind, to leave the house as the care had been in place and working well for Frances. What bill saw as honourable actions, were not condoned by others in the family, namely his two sisters and Frances' relatives. His sisters, who lived in Crewe, disowned him.

In 2015, Frances passed away and the local Red Cross office sent a message to all the charitable institutions in London. This note urged the location of 'Old Bill' the veteran who was blind, to notify him of her passing and urging him to attend her funeral. It worked and a Salvation Army officer, who had come to know Bill, kindly offered to escort him to Crewe, paying all costs. He was taken to a centre where he was given a makeover and general tidy. The officer noticed a small pouch in Bill's inside pocket which held a heavy item. Without showing it, Bill could only explain that he had kept it as a lucky charm. It had arrived in his lap when sitting in a shop doorway many years ago. The charm seemed to have worked as he had not experienced too many hardships since then.

The ceremony was brief with only a dozen or so present. Bill, his two sisters, who kept their distance, some of Frances' relatives, a carer, who had nursed Frances and a members of the local Red Cross Branch. All felt sorry for Bill, except his sisters. Just as the service was ending, the Red Cross officer stood and spoke. He went on to explain what had made Bill leave the home when he did. The told how Bill had kept in regular touch, scribbling a love letter every week and having it posted to their office in Crewe to be handed to Frances his beloved wife. At least every month, included with one of the letters, was a postal order for some reasonable sum to buy Frances a treat.

The Salvation Army Officer then stood to speak. He explained how one of their staff had first met Bill many years ago and offered to help him with his requests. Bill would write his note at the army centre and they would post it for him. He requested that the letter be sent 'care of' a local charity, preferably the Red Cross. Bill would hand over most of the money he had collected together with some of his benefits for them to obtain the postal order. He pleaded with them not to reveal his whereabouts. The officer then explained a little about Bill. When serving in a Middle East conflict, Bill had rescued six of his men from ambush before finally being blinded by a shell. The VC which hung around his neck gave credit for his heroic actions.

Captain William (Bill) Fareleigh, now stood from where he sat. He firstly explained how he never spoke of the tragic incidents in the conflict and how many of his comrades had been lost. He was grateful for having the courage to rescue six of his men from ambush and would do it all again, even if loss of his sight resulted. His mind was continually plagued by those friends who passed away.

He then recalled his times with Frances and how much he loved her. All were brought to tears, as water welled from his eyelids when he explained why he felt he had to go away. When he returned, a blind man, the doctors gave him no hope of ever seeing again. He was distraught to learn of Frances' condition. He was told that she had dementure, continual fits happening every two hours, twenty four hours a day. She had a live in carer and whilst her hearing was reasonable, she had lost all power to speak. Bill could not place any more worry onto his adored wife and thus he decided to find his own way. Writing his letters had given him reason to live and he thanked the Red Cross and Salvation Army for all their support. After giving his speech, Bill collapsed onto the floor with a thud.

One of his sisters came to help him. Bill had, as usual, hidden the VC and chain inside his vest, however, the chain had snagged as he fell. This, in turn, dislodged the small leather pouch from his inside pocket. The pouch fell also to the floor and the bracelet dropped clear. Gasps of air intake followed as the sister came closer to examine the charm, ignoring Bill. He regained his senses as the bracelet was now being closely examined by his sisters. When asked how he had come to have it, he explained it's origin and how he had kept it as his lucky charm for all these years, hidden from view.

Within ten minutes, the sisters had determined Bill's future and were insisting he should come to live in their small house in Crewe and leave the streets of London in the past. This reminded Bill of why he lived as a nomad, moving from place to place in London and requesting the Army not to reveal his whereabouts, at any time, to his family. He feared they would take him back to live with his dreaded sisters. Having lost his love, Bill was overcome with emotion. He was now being conveted by his remaining family. They persuaded him.

Twenty-four hours went by and then it started. Arguments as to who should wear, it then who should own it. the elder claiming that she should have it. All thoughts of their promises to look after Bill had taken a back seat. Beryl held it clasped to her heart and after much pleading, her younger sister Evelyn accepted. Beryl put the bracelet on her wrist and immediately Eve noticed that her sister's appearance improved.

Beryl had seen young Philip in town on a few dates, nothing serious, he didn't seem that keen. She rang him that evening to arrange to meet at the usual pub for a drink. When Philip saw Beryl, he could not believe this was the same lady. She looked ten years younger and her face was full of charm and beauty. He wondered why he had not been keen on her all these months. After a few drinks, the couple left to see a late-night movie at the local cinema.

Julian had been drinking far too much. He was a bad driver when sober and had received two warnings for using his mobile whilst driving. This particular evening, he had started with a drink with Philip before moving to the pool table for a few games with the lads. When Beryl turned up, he was very envious. He cursed his luck as he had been out with her, before she met with Philip after he ditched her. He was a more than happy man though after downing two whiskeys and two more pints before he got into his Land Rover. He raced off to his girlfriend's flat in anticipation of a 'friendly' half hour. He didn't stay very long. His girlfriend smelled the drink and tried to persuade him to stay the night after scolding him. Julian decided he did not want to stay with all the nagging and decided to return home to play live casino games on his iPad. After satisfying his lust, he made his excuses and sped off. His route would take him past the cinema. Just as he approached that area, doing fifty miles per hour, his phone rang. He took it from his chest pocket and saw it was Lucy, his girlfriend. He pressed the accept button and WHAM. He swerved onto the pavement and struck Beryl and Philip head on. The poor lady was gone. So was the charm from her wrist. The charm which Philip had so admired over the past two hours.

CITANDUM PER ADVERSUM COLLEM PERICULOSUM

❖

Speeding Up a Hill Is Dangerous

George was a loose cannon and had no ties at all in his life. He often visited Crewe to meet up with some pals who were also keen on vintage cars. He was shocked when he saw the Land Rover out of control and hit the couple. He pulled over, but realised there was nothing he could do to help and there were other witnesses to the incident who were also exiting the cinema. What caught his interest was something in the gutter. The lights from his car and those from the cinema caught a bright gleam. He jumped from his perfectly restored Morris and held the golden bracelet before slipping it into his corduroy jacket pocket. He would not have known the history of his find and how it had affected all who wore it.

The time George spent in Crewe had been very interesting, not only for the stories told by his mates, but also for a personal challenge. He was asked to call in to see a sister of one guy, who lived on her own in Bath. This was quite convenient, as George lived in Foxhill, just outside the city on one of the surrounding hills. It was late to start his journey but the Morris driver preferred to travel at night. Less traffic and therefore less stress and less pressure on his beloved car from all those lorries pushing him along, as was always the case during daytime driving. After two stops on route, he finally arrived home and relished the thought of spending at least two weeks there before going North for a vintage car show on the Wirral.

He only slept for a few hours and mid-afternoon he was determined to head into the city to call on his friend's sister, Cheryl. He had seen her photograph and was very impressed with her appearance. A bonus was her ownership of a little bistro which she had established five years ago and was flourishing. Following a phone call, all was arranged for George to park up in a special area near the bistro and call in for a coffee. He enjoyed the drink, but enjoyed the hostess even more. Cheryl was quite impressed with George because of his adventurous attitude and likeable manner. When told that she enjoyed Italian operas, George immediately broke into 'Che Gelida Manina 'from La Boheme and this impressed Cheryl very much. It didn't take much persuasion for

Cheryl to agree to go for a short ride in George's Morris. She told her assistant to look after things for a few hours and trotted out with her new admirer for a short adventure. As soon as they were seated, George could not resist. He took out the bracelet and placed it on the wrist of his beautiful passenger. The route out of the city centre involved a steep climb through busy streets. The traffic that day was far busier than normal and as they approached the final stretch, which was one way, in their favour, they came to a halt. This section was lined with the most popular shops and restaurants in Bath and there were always hundreds of tourists crossing back and forth, one of the reasons the council made this a one-way stretch of roadway. Cheryl was completely overwhelmed with the wonder of the charm. Her face glowed with excitement as she continuously examined it. So much so, that she had forgotten to fasten her seat belt. It also didn't register as the car was stopped often as they tried to proceed up the steep hill. George had fitted seat belts when he spent three thousand pounds on general upgrades of his treasured Morris, but no warning system was added.

The traffic lights had changed three times and they had moved up only about six car spaces. They were on red and their car stopped, as dozens of shoppers began crossing in between cars to cross from either side. A young lady with a child in a buggy were walking directly in front of the Morris.

George had noticed several cars behind him had turned off this road looking for an alternative route. He glanced in his rear view mirror to see a black Mercedes speeding to fill that space. The car was going extremely fast and had no driver. In situations such as this, sometimes the human brain can react quickly, George acted very quickly.

His immediate concern was the young lady with the buggy. He doubled the tension on the handbrake, slammed his foot on the footbrake, banged his horn, flashed his lights, wound down his window and shouted and screamed with all his might. All this in a split second and prayed for things to be okay, then waited for the impact.

The crunch came. The lady and buggy had rushed clear. His car was pushed towards the tailgate of the lorry in front of him. He ducked under the steering wheel only to see Cheryl's head go crashing through the windscreen and her body follow. His door had buckled and he could only get out through the passenger door. When he got to Cheryl, he could see that there was no hope for her. The damage to her head alone was substantial. He lept from the bonnet and turned to the Merc. The driver was now sitting upright behind an air-bag. To his left and crouching in the front passenger well, was a child, a boy no older than four. Next to the child was a mobile phone, switched on with a voice talking into space. George always carried a pen knife on his belt to assist with the ever-needed jobs on his Morris and any other D.I.Y. He pierced the air-bag and dragged the driver into the road. The man was crying and in a terrible state. Thoughts of exacting a swift revenge and beating the Merc driver abated as the weeping continued together with cries of anguish. Tim Saunders, Chairman of a major Company name in retail, thought he had killed his only son. George calmed and told him that he thought he might be ok, as he was lying in the well, safe he believed, from serious injury. The driver also calmed and began his explanation.

He noticed that a gap of about forty metres suddenly appeared as cars were turning off to the left. As he increased speed, he saw in his mirror, his little boy climb out of his child seat in the rear and crawl between the two front seats. He realised he had not secured him correctly with the straps. This always gave him a problem. Suddenly, his phone rang. He panicked, dropped the phone and tried to reach down to his boy, who by now was in the front passenger seat crawling into the well. All this took place in about three to four seconds. What really made matters worse was the driver putting his foot on the accelerator instead of the brake.

It was at this point that George had looked through his rear-view mirror to see no driver visible.

Within an hour of the incident, the emergency services had managed to sort everything. Cheryl's brother had been informed and he was on his way. Meanwhile, the Morris had been towed to a local garage and George was having a coffee at Tim's mansion. George was still in shock, when he suddenly remembered the bracelet. It was not on her wrist as she was put into the ambulance. His mind was in turmoil and he became so agitated that very soon he was taken to the hospital by ambulance. He would not find peace for many months.

ELEVENTH CHAIN LINK

SERPENS ALATA PAVOREM CREAT

———◆◇◆———

A Winged Serpent Creates Horror

It was fate, which saw the bracelet follow George to that mansion. When things had been sorted following the crash, Tim suggested that George go home with him and his son in a cab. Tim wanted to thank George for remaining calm and not insisting on Police taking any action. He did reward George with a cheque for ten thousand pounds to cover repairs to his Morris. Whilst George put this into an inside pocket, he would not recall it for a while. When Cheryl was Jettisoned through the windscreen, the bracelet had come away and flung backwards over the Morris roof. It had lodged into the front grill of the Mercedes. Tim's brother ran a garage in Bath and on request, had towed the car back to Tim's so he could sort the contents before having it taken away for repairs.

Little Matthew was full of beans and not being injured was very enquiring as to the damage to the Car. Whilst he was looking at the grill, he noticed something very shiny and plucked the charm away and handed it to his Mother. All this unknown by his Father or George who were taking tea and chatting in the lounge. Mrs Saunders was finalising her packing, as she was about to travel to the USA to visit her Sister. Clare Saunders' Sister was married to an engineer who worked for the US Navy at a base in Groton Connecticut on the East Coast. Clare hated flying, but her Sister was very poorly and she felt that this visit might be the last time she might see her. Her mind was on many things as the bracelet was brought to her by her son. She straight away put it into her handbag and for some reason, did not tell anyone about it. It would be some days before Tim found out about this incident.

The journey to Groton entailed flying to New York, then onwards by a short hop to Hartford springs. The latter flight was usually in a small prop aircraft and about sixteen to twenty passengers was the norm. This flight, being so frequent, could have its problems and, it was a little over stretched. Clare had done this trip only once before, however, that had seen a strange incident. Whilst the aircraft was taxiing ready for take-off, there was a loud banging near the rear. Clare had shouted for the attendant to investigate. There was only one stewardess on board.

After several urges, she finally came down from the front, were she was seated, to check. She shouted for the pilot to halt as she proceeded to open the rear door. Someone was trying to get on board, having missed the official boarding time. Apparently, this had happened on a prior occasion. So, this service was more alike to a bus service or coach service, as it was so regular. Anything goes on this schedule.

At about the same time as George was looking at his 'blood money' in Bath, Clare decided to put on the bracelet before her flight to Hartford Springs. She had examined it several times during the long-haul flight from UK and had pondered donating it to Julie. However, she was very impressed with the charm and had decided to keep it. As she put it on her wrist, she seemed to become calmer as her flight was called.

Clare settled into seat 6f, a window seat and a young lady came to sit next to her. Clare was not wanting to chat; however, this did not deter the student next to her. The flight was only about one hour and having to talk with somebody, would, she thought make the time pass more quickly. For the first ten minutes, the young lady insisted on recalling all the bad experiences she had on this, her regular flight from New York. She studied in Groton, where she lived with her boyfriend.

One occasion when the inside window came away in her hand as she touched it. Another when a passenger walked up the aisle holding two arm rests which had come away as he was fastening his seat belt. A further story of a loud crashing noise as the door of an overhead locker fell into a seat – thankfully empty at the time.

Clare became nervous, recalling her prior experience and beads of sweat appeared on her brow. Thoughts and concerns that this aircraft might not be maintained properly, occupied her brain. Clare disliked the idea of flying as she was afraid of heights and the thought that there was little chance of survival in an air crash. She ignored all the statistics regarding percentages compared to driving etc and insisted on cruises when holidaying with Tim and more recently, Matthew.

She was gripping her bracelet very tightly when the student gave some concern regarding the direction of their flight. Normally she was informed, and Clare could not remember from her only previous flight, from take-off, the aircraft headed North, in the same direction as the runway. Then after a few minutes, turned slightly to the left and continued over land. The student explained that, it was only a short flight, there were plenty of sites of interest as they began to climb, and she was looking forward to seeing them over again. This flight, however, after only two or three minutes in the air, began to turn to the right heading over water.

A short blast on the intercom and the pilot made an announcement. "Ladies and gentlemen, we have a fire in the rear right engine. I am returning to the airport after shedding some excess fuel over the bay".

The last four years of Clare's life flashed by: her husband admitting to having an affair with his secretary, Clare drinking two bottles of wine a day, smoking sixty cigarettes culminating in heart problems, daily medication.

Following the announcement, there was an immediate silence for one second. THEN all hell broke loose. There were only fourteen passengers on the flight and all bar one gave out sounds. Some screamed in terror, some poured endearment to their loved ones, some prayed, the student next to Clare screamed for help as she dropped her iPad, pleading for somebody to retrieve it. Madness in all. Clare sat in silence, the bracelet gone from her wrist. As the student fumbled blindly on the floor, she grasped the charm and placed it into her purse.

The aircraft was met by half a dozen fire engines and several ambulances. Ten minutes after landing and following immediate checks, it was found to have a fault in the wiring panel. There was no fire, but the Captain had taken the right action. The airline kept the thirteen passengers in the departure lounge expecting them to re-board the same aircraft. Two hours later, they were asked to commence boarding. All refused and demanded another aircraft, especially as there had been a cadaver on seat 6f.

TWELFTH CHAIN LINK
CAVE MOTUS REPENTINOS ADVERSUS TE

❖❖❖

Beware of Sudden Movements Towards You

T he young student was Italian and was planning to return to her parents when her course was complete. She had no intention of making her boyfriend a permanent fixture and the incident enabled her decision to cut short her stay in the USA and go home. She did not wear the charm, but often examined it and thought she could make some sense of the minute inscriptions when looking through a magnifying glass. Andrea was so pleased to see her Father waiting for her as she exited through the 'nothing to declare' gate at Trieste airport. The drive could take only about two hours mainly due to the speed they would travel. Marco, her Father had recently purchased a black Mercedes, top of the range for one hundred and thirty thousand euros. His business in producing quality fabrics was doing exceptionally well and future prospects were bright. Andrea's education in materials and design would surely provide additional benefit and boost income.

As she sat in the luxurious passenger seat, Andrea took out the charm, showed it to her Father and fastened it onto her wrist. She explained that the links and clasp appeared to be inscribed minutely in Latin. Her Father told her that he knew a jeweller who might be able to examine it and determine more. He was impressed with it and having a close look before they set off, he noted a word! DEVA Which he knew to have been an early Roman settlement in North West England. Marco suggested it might be extremely valuable and told Andrea that it suited her very much, and her boyfriend was very generous buying it for her.

They sped onto the motorway, with Andrea giving a slight smile, knowing that her Father had believed her story of how the young man from New England had been so much in love with her, so much so that he had insisted she accept the bracelet which had been given to him by his Grandmother. This in the hope that Andrea would keep in touch and email him when she arrived home.

All was going so well in the lives of Andrea and her Father as they cruised along the motorway at one hundred and ten kilometres per hour.

Thirty minutes into their journey they saw, what appeared to be, a puff of smoke from the central reservation about half a mile ahead. The stretch of motorway now was straight, just as a Roman road. There was hardly any traffic in front of them, so Marco slowed only slightly on seeing the smoke. Within a few seconds, a long straight piece of heavy metal was bouncing towards them at speed. Horror, it was a lamppost and it sped past them to their left, missing their car by inches. What happened over the following sixty seconds seemed a dream to Andrea. In fact, it was to be her worse ever nightmare.

Marco brought the Merc to a halt, still in the fast lane. Within a few seconds after the lamppost had shot past, a very large, twin trailer vehicle approached on the inside lane going backwards on their side of the motorway. There was no traffic in front apart from this and the vehicle went past them at about twenty kilometres per hour, with the driver slumped over his wheel. It became clear that this driver had crossed over the central reservation, then after dislodging the lamppost, which turned him round, he went backwards along the road. Marco and Andrea were breathing a sigh of relief at avoiding this collision when without warning, a tailgate of a low loader crashed into their passenger window and started taking them forward along the motorway. Andrea managed to duck into the well, as the lorry caught the vertical stanchion. She was now pinned and unable to move. They were unaware that the driver of this low loader was only the first of many to be hit by the twin vehicle continuing its journey backwards.

Marco smelled petrol. It was dripping from the tank which was now lodged above the passenger seat area, with Andrea crouched and trapped beneath. After being hauled forward for about 50 meters the conjoined car and lorry came to a halt. The terrible sounds of screams and crunching metal filled the air. Father and daughter looked about to see if there was any escape, especially for the daughter.

From what started as a drip, the petrol now began to flow more freely from the ruptured tank and small pools began to develop in the well around Andrea. Marco was trying very hard to rescue his beloved daughter, to no avail. His door had also been damaged during the incident and his only means of escape was to climb somehow into the back. He then saw several large black oil drums blocking this route, drums which must have crashed from the flat back through his car window. Marco did not lose hope. He recalled stories of how, when faced with adversity, miracles can happen and humans can achieve super strengths. As he began to pull at the heavy drums it happened. A spark! Oh God no, please no, please please no. Why us? Why now? God would not answer this time, stronger forces were taking control.

He would not leave his daughter. They both perished.

When the rescue services: police, fire and ambulance arrived, they were horrified at the carnage caused by the twin trailer driver falling asleep at his wheel, 20 dead and 100 vehicles destroyed. The worst scene was inside the black Mercedes. All grieved at what they saw, the charred remains of father and daughter holding hands.

The driver who caused all this horror survived, was charged with manslaughter and jailed for 10 years, the maximum penalty at that time.

Unnoticed by everyone following the clearing of the disaster, was a glint of light shining through the tall grasses and rubble on the central reservation. It seems that in his efforts to pull Andrea free, he had grasped the charm and unknowingly wrenched it from her wrist. The bracelet lay there for several days and it was a relative of Andrea who found it,

Nina, spotted it as she was laying some flowers at the scene where the Car had caught fire and ended the lives of her father and sister. She risked her own life rushing to and from that spot as the traffic was quite heavy. As soon as she saw it, Nina placed the charm into her shoulder bag and raced back to Riccardo, her boyfriend, who waited, parked on the hard shoulder.

When he was later shown the bracelet, Ricci gave a knowing smile. Nina was not aware that Andrea had previously owned it and was also unaware that Ricci was planning to go away with Andrea on her return. Andrea had phoned him on arrival at the airport and texted a photo of the charm which she said might provide for them both. No-one in the family had suspected their secret desires, especially the younger sister, Nina. Poor Nina was totally in love with handsome Riccardo, and she was oblivious to all the emails and texts that were sent between him and her sister. Love often blossoms in the written word and Ricci was a true romantic with a persuasive use of words.

The fact that Riccardo didn't seem very upset at the loss of Andrea though, meant that more thoughts of being together came from the female. Riccardo could, therefore, be classed as a cad. He was so full of his self admiration that he could never have related any of the unfortunate and terrible events as having any connection with the bracelet. The specially formed charm which continued to cause danger to those who wore it.

Nina and Riccardo arrived back to Lucia, who was still grief stricken from the loss of her husband and daughter. Nina, also extremely tearful gave up the charm to her mother in a hope that it may bring just a little pleasure, even for a short while. Her mother thanked her and without really looking at it, put the charm in the top drawer of the living room cabinet. Riccardo, on the other hand made a note of exactly where the gleaming item had been placed.

THIRTEENTH CHAIN LINK

NOCTE IN FLEXU VIAE LENTE ITE

◆◆◆◆

go slowly on a bend at night

Many months went by and following a cold and bitter winter, the warmth of spring arrived. Light, at long last, shone through the finally parted curtains into the living room where the bracelet still lay, in anticipation of the next adventure. By this time, Riccardo had been very much accepted as part of the family. He was given a set of keys to the house, helped the two ladies in maintaining the property and large gardens. The gardens had extensive lawns and borders and Riccardo went about his chores with enthusiasm. He planted many flowers and shrubs and all were looking forward to summer. Riccardo had additional talents which included not only his handsome frame but also his piano and singing skills. He did not stay overnight during the weekdays, however, and kept to his routine of 2-4 hours each weekday and many more hours over the weekends.

During these times he could not take his mind from the gleam of the bracelet. When he was alone and certain of not being disturbed, he would sneak a glimpse into the drawer. On each occasion he became convinced that the charm was wasting away being hidden as it was. As the summer wore on, Riccardo could not contain his lust any longer, not for Nina but for that charm.

It occurred one Sunday evening in late August. He was performing the opening aria from La Boheme, - Che Gelida Manila. This was Nina's favourite and salt water welled from her eyes. Her mother, Lucia, was also brought to tears, remembering the losses earlier that year. This rendition was by far, his best ever performance even surprising himself. It was as if he were inspired, no errors and an audience would be truly impressed. Any of the popular Tenors would have commended his work.

Riccardo sat, exhausted. What all did not appreciate was that this was to be his final performance and his farewell. The ladies agreed that Riccardo must stay over that evening, especially Nina, who relished the chance to spend many hours in her lover's arms. Lucia was pleased that her daughter had found an honourable man and was looking forward to their engagement.

Riccardo slipped from the bed, looking back at Nina, completely satisfied and deep in slumber. It was 3am and he had decided on this move immediately after he had completed his aria. Satisfied that Lucia was also asleep, he crept downstairs and into the living room, carrying his clothes. Within minutes, he dressed with the bracelet secure in the inside breast pocket of his leather jacket. He opened the front door, stepped out into the fresh morning air and then turned to post his letter back through the letter box. He had locked the door but had forgotten to leave the note on the living room table. He felt sure they would find it, albeit after a short while. Finally, he posted the house keys. He felt a little guilty: not only had he originally planned to cheat on Nina, but now he was a thief. Would he ever be forgiven. The answer, in his mind was - no.

He departed from that house in the knowledge that he would never return, but not for any obvious reasons. No - one could envisage what events would surround the final 3 links and then, the clasp.

Riccardo had relatives in Sorrento. It took him several days, as he stopped en route, in Rome, to meet up with a friend. An acquaintance, a pretty lady who owned a Pizzeria, not far from The Trevi Fountain. Being a budding lothario, Ricci had a girl in nearly all the major cities and Maria had known him for several years. He kept in touch by phone and text and she was pleased when advised he was on his way to see her. Even more so when he said he was on his way to Sorrento and wanted her to join him. He was a fortunate young man, his uncle owned a small, but extemely popular hotel on the slopes overlooking the bay. Maria suggested they stay one night in her flat in Rome and enjoy the evening, having a late meal in one of the squares. Whilst Ricci showed the bracelet, he did not invite Maria to put it on her wrist until they had lain together in their room in Sorrento.

Their room overlooked the steep slopes descending to the town and bay. The setting was very romantic, with a balcony to enjoy the evening lights and sounds lifting gently from below. Maria's face glowed with appreciation as she put on the charm. Her skin was tanned and most of the guests who glanced over as the couple entered the dining room, commented on how glamorous the young lady looked. Most of the guests that evening were from the USA and everyone noticed the gleam of the bracelet on Maria's wrist. Following the meal, a very small local man provided some entertainment, singing with his guitar. Many of the songs were slightly distorted Versions of Elvis classics.

A tour guide arrived, as planned by the American visitors, to escort them into town to spend the evening in a famous theatre, near the coast. This excursion was extremely popular with visitors to Sorrento and the arrangement included drinks in the adjoining courtyard, which overlooked the bay, prior to enjoying the excellent musical which was always performing there. Two coaches had been arranged and there was room for 2 more passengers. Uncle Paolo knew the guide and after confirming with the couple, he paid for them to join in the evening entertainment as a special treat. The only additional costs for them would be any drinks taken in the courtyard bars which sold almost every tipple conceivable for the theatre guest to select.

Within 30 minutes, the coaches arrived at the hotel, to transport all down the very steep and winding narrow road into town.This road was hazardous and had seen many incidents over the years. The sharp bends were reinforced on the open slope side with strong metal spikes, connected by wire mesh netting. Three of these bends were particularly dangerous, however., they were well signposted and all local drivers were aware of them. Another hazard was the width of the road. It was built in Roman times and had hardly been widened over the many centuries. There were passing points, but not many. This road was one of the reasons why only a few hotels had been built in this area. Also, there were not many houses. This reduced the amount of traffic, fortunately, for those who used this perilous route. Paolo had made many requests for road improvements, but the town committee had many more priorities which would bring additional tourist revenues.

The Americans and the couple were extremely impressed with the courtyard area alongside the theatre. There was an excellent view of the Bay and it was quite spacious. The Terrace, as the theatre owner preferred to call it, was an ideallic scene. Coloured lighting, ample seating and tables, four bars to ensure very little queuing for drinks or refreshments. A quartet of musicians provided exceptional music, extracts from Puccini's operas. It was a truly romantic setting and Ricci could see that Maria was warming to him and was holding him closer at each glance. The bracelet shone very brightly, it was enjoying it's longevity in this country.

The vino Rosso and vino bianco flowed freely at very reasonable prices and the dry, warm evening air provided, together with the vista, the perfect setting. The bell sounded and all made their way into the theatre foyer. The coach drivers were also allowed entry with the special passes issued to them. One of the drivers from the Hotel Paolo, however, did not want to watch the show as he preferred entertainment of a very different kind. He had very little interest in musicals, opera or such things, he preferred the night life found in several of the narrow alleyways in the town centre. He remained on the terrace looking at the ferries and the expensive yachts sailing back and forth to Capri. It was indeed, a beautiful scene and so was the middle aged lady who sat in one of the shaded areas near a bar. She wore a loose fitting red dress which had a plunging neckline and she beckoned the driver to join her. Luigi knew that to take even a sip of alcohol during working hours was a serious offence and demanded summary dismissal and he also knew that he had a return journey to make to the hotel later. He was a romantic and was too easily swayed by a good looking lady. This was no ordinary lady. Rosa knew how to excite her prey. Although in her late 50's, her speciality and desire was to have a conquest on the terrace each time she visited the theatre, which was at least twice each month. Her successes included pop stars, politicians and business moguls from every continent. Tonight though, it would be the turn of a handsome, young coach driver.

Her plan and long term project was, one day, to write a memoir of all her terrace experiences which, she felt, would be a best seller. She had toyed with the idea of actually naming and putting into chronological order all her conquests.

Luigi had one glass of rosso, a small glass, before he began his allowed 15 minutes of passion. Only 15 minutes at which time Rosa would declare "Finito". What he did not realise was that a small love potion had been dropped into his glass. A secret herbal mixture which would immediately increase his blood lust and within 30 minutes would make his overall senses weaker for several hours.

The show finished and after 5 encores everyone left to go to the terrace, make their way to the town centre or return home. Luigi and the other driver greeted their passengers and shortly began their trip back up to the hotel. Everybody noticed that Luigi seemed particularly happy. On the route up the steep inclines two things happened.

Firstly, the heavens opened. A cloud burst of terrific proportion with torrents of water gushing down along the narrow unlit roadway. It appeared like a river was suddenly flowing.

Secondly, Luigi began rubbing his eyes. He started to feel tired and losing concentration.

He managed a few of the tight bends and was about half way up when it happened. A mud slide, and instead of pulling in towards the hill face and then stopping, Luigi tried to drive on, sending the coach crashing through the metal chain link and over the slope. Riccardo and Maria were seated at the back and were sensing the peril on this journey. Ricci had shouted several times for the driver to stop, to no avail. Just as the coach started to slide Ricci grabbed the rear door emergency handle and whilst opening it, pulled Maria onto the roadway. The two lovers stood and watched in disbelief as the coach overturned, threw two more passengers clear, then continued to tumble down the steep hillside.

Screams filled the air as the rain subsided, the coach only finally stopping as it smashed into a small bistro on the winding road below. About a dozen people were seated under an awning, protected from the rain and they took the brunt of the hit. Even then the coach was moving so much that it continued on into the building seriously injuring many more.

A devastating scene and the two held each other tightly as events below unfolded. Ricci reflected on how fortunate they were to be seated in the rear with a large emergency door behind them, enabling their escape. Also, the coach appeared to be just slowing, perhaps Luigi had finally come to his senses? As they stood watching and listening to the screams, they noticed a couple climbing back up the hillside. How they also had been so lucky reflected Maria.

All four pairs of eyes met as a heavy lorry appeared from nowhere, it seemed, and careered into Riccardo and Maria killing them instantly, there was no escape on this occasion.

The bracelet was flung from her wrist as Maria was sent sprawling into the air. It landed just in front of the American couple as they watched in complete terror as the lorry passed by them some 10 metres away. Tony was still in shock and his head hurt badly. He was confused and so pleased to see Annette standing with him showing signs of only bruising to the side of her face. They felt that a miracle had saved them and their faces lit up on seeing the charm laying in all it's splendour in front of them. Tony picked it up and placed it in his bum back along side his cash and cards. He grasped his wife's hand and determined to climb up and back to their hotel.

Paolo and his staff were distressed as the police informed them of events. This had been a devastating incident and it would be some time before the total picture was known. What was certain was that 30 people were killed and more than 20 injured. Among the dead were Riccardo and Maria.

When Tony and Annette crawled in, all were amazed.

FOURTEENTH CHAIN LINK

MASSAS MARMORIS. DEVITATE

◇◆◆◆◇

Keep clear of blocks of marble

Tony woke at 5 am. He held his head in both hands, staring up at the ceiling, as he had done for the past 9 months. Although he had escaped death in Sorrento, he had suffered severe headaches and after shock. Annette, on the other hand, was suffering from amnesia, a condition which was common following a near death experience. Her brain had locked away all memory of that devastating evening and only when she was strong enough would her memory return. Tony was due for his second scan which, hopefully, would reveal the cause of his problems. He felt he could not continue his life in the manner he now lived. He was a senior partner in a leading firm of architects in New York and whilst the board appreciated his condition, they were beginning to mutter complaints regarding his continued absense.

The second scan results proved beneficial. Doctors were able to identify the causes and prescribe a remedy for the pains. The treatment was available from a French Pharmaceutical company and had proven success with 3 prior similar cases.

Within three months of treatment, the headaches had subsided and the nervous condition due to aftershock were no longer apparent. He began to gather himself together and was able to relive that fateful evening in Italy. He went to the wardrobe and emptied the suitcase of the remaining items following their return all those months ago. Tucked away was a small leather pouch, inside which he found the bracelet. On their return, Tony's mother had been very helpful. Whilst unpacking their belongings, she had overlooked this small pouch which would give the couple hope for their future.

Tony's eyes lit up. What a find. He was now able to examine the charm in more detail. He could not decipher the minute inscriptions, however, he felt that this was a valuable piece. He immediately thought of showing it to Annette, as it may help her remember events and bring her some relief. As he placed the bracelet around his wife's wrist, he did not notice the flickering and sparkle in her eyes. This was to be the trigger needed by her brain to create a reaction. Within 5 minutes,

Annette was weeping tears of joy as she held Tony and placed her head on his chest.

Members of the board were very pleased for the couple. Their joint recovery was amazing and everyone in the company looked forward to Tony's return. They were somewhat disappointed when he requested a Two week extension to his present bout of absense. He advised that he wanted to take his wife away from it all to relish the sudden recovery, somewhere far away. Following a great deal of deliberation, he persuaded his wife to venture to Indonesia. Tony had been there on business some years previous and was told of the many exotic places to visit. He had no time to indulge in such pleasures and vowed to return one day. Annette was especially keen on exotic birds and fish and there were places in that country which had abundance of both. Her mind was easily persuaded also due to the influence being exerted by the charm, to leave the apparent safety of their home.

Their itinerary was organised by one of the contacts, an agent known to Tony called Bang Din. His plan was to spend a few days in Jakarta, then drive north to Bandung, this journey to include a visit to one of the most naturalised zoos in the Southern Hemisphere. This area included hundreds of exotic birds, many only living in this tropical paradise. Both Tony and Marie were enthusiasts in these species and this was probably the main reason for arranging this holiday. The zoo keeper was a close friend of the agent and promised to make their trip extremely memorable.

On arrival at their five star hotel in Jakarta, Tony reflected, for a few minutes, on his previous visit. He had wanted to know more about life in this dynamic country and to understand more, how the ordinary people lived. His agent suggested they went into the suburbs not very far from their hotel, where he could experience how the average working person dined. He also made Tony aware that he might be somewhat shocked at some of the events. There was a big divide in the country - the haves and the have nots.

The local expedition, as Bang Din referred to it, would take only an hour or so. On reaching the main road exiting north, they stopped at lights only for the car to be besieged by scantily dressed men and women begging at their windows for money. These unfortunates were dispersed by four fully armed police. Within seconds and before the lights changed, a group of about a dozen children appeared carrying empty cereal boxes pleading for handouts. The agent explained that these families lived in the open sewers which were the only places for them to stay. Resolving this would be the next project for the ruling President to address in Government on his return from vacation in Bali.He had made this promise on numerous other occasions, the obstacles included the fact that no-one would take responsibility for the unfortunates and certainly nobody wanted them as neighbours. Relocation was almost impossible.

Within ten minutes, they had parked in a local shopping area and were seated in a busy, noisy restaurant. There were ten in all seated at the large circular table and Tony went with the flow regarding the meal selection. Within minutes, ten plates were brought to them and placed, not in any sense or order, onto the table. None of the food was recognisable and no cutlery was made available. An obvious finger buffet thought Tony, as he picked up and started to chew on a grey piece of smooth looking meat. He thought it was foul and carefully replaced it on his side plate and began to chew on another portion which looked only slightly healthier. No, this was equally bad, so back on his small dish, this went. So after trying all Ten dishes and only swallowing one, Tony advised that he was satisfied and wished to leave. The waiter was called and proceeded to take copious notes on examining his and the agent's plates. Bang Din explained that they would only be charged for what they had eaten. What remained on their plates would be taken back to the kitchen, washed then re-issued on plates for other customers. So this was how the poor survived. When Tony dared to ask what he had eaten or tasted, in particular his first try, he was informed that it was indeed fried lung. Also, he realised that he had probably chewed on and tasted food which had been through similar trials. Tony was violently sick into the nearby open sewer.

Another, more pleasing memory, was watching troops of young school children, well dressed, walking in file along the streets to school. The future was looking brighter. The schedules for rebuilding and re- housing were substantial and Tony's company had been selected to be involved in these and the vast Industrial development.

It was bright and sunny in the morning that the trio set off north from Jakarta, not realising what lay ahead. The couple had dined in a renowned fish bar the previous evening and the marinated prawns had given them a surprising experience. Gifts were awarded to any visitors who dined for the first time and managed to eat all the prawns presented on the highly decorated plates. Both Tony and Annette liked prawns and the test was an easy "pass" for them both. Their gift was a bottle of a wonderful herbal liqueur which included an aphrodisiac. They had a sensual evening back at the hotel, the best night together for many many months.

The Land Rover turned off the main road after an hour. The zoo was even more interesting than the brochure depicted. It was more akin to an animal reserve with rhinos and elephants roaming freely. Armed personnel drove about keeping keen eyes on the visitors, the prey, and the beasts. The aviary, housing hundreds of tropical birds was substantial and the couple spent 3 hours in this area. Annette knew that her video would be well received by all members of her club on return. Life was changing and happiness for the future seemed assured. The bracelet was gleaming ever brighter.

In the 2 years since Tony's previous visit, a marble mine had been started on the way to Bandung. This mine was proving successful and although not fully developed, and the appropriate investment secured, excavation was well underway. The problem at the time the Land Rover was approaching was that open flat back lorries were being used for transport. Cut into approximately 6 ft cubes, the marble was loaded then secured by strapping. The hazard was the exit as the roadway had been subject to extreme wear and tear and it was quite narrow. As with many such projects in the country, not enough thought had been given to the support network and road structure at the outset, although plans were underway to sort these issues.

Bang Din knew that, whilst the marble blocks were cut into cubes and therefore assisting stability, the strapping could not possibly hold the huge weight in place if there was movement. He therefore kept at least 3/4 car lengths behind for additional safety. He was reflecting on these things when a fully loaded flat back pulled out of the mine just ahead.

This would add considerable time to their journey and a late arrival in Bandung. Caution was paramount on one particular bend. This was almost 90* and included the roots of a huge tree which projected through the rock face. On the outer side of the road there was a shear drop of about 200 ft into the valley where the mine was located. There were similar areas around the world and as an example, along the Amalfi coast in Italy, strong wire meshing is positioned and secured along the rock face, to help hold it all in place. The Indonesian government were playing catch up with preventative measures and this particular bend was about to be sorted. The problem was that the surveyors had not realised the extent of the deterioration caused by these heavily laden lorries and the affect on the exposed roots.

This all became so evident as the lorry driver, that day, in his effort to keep well away from the slope, clipped several of the protruding roots

It sounded like a cannon. Coinciding with two of the straps splitting, a huge lump of rock crashed from the area above the damaged roots. It was impossible to avoid and all three in the Land Rover were crushed instantly without feeling any pain. At the same instant, the lorry swayed and the unbalanced large cube of marble slid from the flat back. The lorry driver could hardly believe his eyes as he watched the cube, the lorry and the Land Rover tumble, in turn, over the edge. He had managed to jump clear on hearing the explosion of sound. Screams could be heard as the wreckage and marble tumbled into the groups working below. Chang rang the emergency services to alert them of the terrible incident. As he spoke, his eyes caught the gleam from a golden bracelet, laying on the roadway, having been flung from a wrist in the crush. More than 12 had been killed in all and 20 injured.

105 AD.

The meretrix,[6] whose name was Metella, decided not to wear the bracelet but to hide it under her skirts. This would be a long journey and she was worried about robbers attacking her to steal the golden charm. Her thoughts were of re-uniting with her lover and provider, Crassus. He had ordered her to go to Londinium, under escort, to spend seven fruitful days with his close friend, the centurion Augustini. Metella was the most voluptuous of all the ladies in the brothel and Augustini was keen to see her, having heard so much about her from Crassus. Even though she had pleased him in every way possible, the centurion proved too forceful. He became too violent on each occasion she gave herself to him. The arrangement was for 7 days and Metella was overjoyed when he explained that he was being recalled to Rome. So, after 3 days she was allowed to return to Deva, however, with only one of the escorts to accompany her. She felt that Crassus would not be pleased to learn of the two deserters and would arrange for their demise when told. She knew that she was a valuable asset to him and would not want her harmed. Augustini was angry at his leaving so soon for Rome, he had sent 20 gold denarii in advance to Crassus for the lady's presence.

Whilst, initially, the meretrix was pleased to be free from the brutish centurion, she became extremely anxious about her lone escort. On the journey south, Theodore had made unwelcome advances towards her, but his comrades had warned him of the consequences if Crassus discovered she had been violated. The first approach was made only 2 hours from leaving Londinium. Metella was tending to the horse, which was pulling the small carriage, as it appeared slightly lame. She had a good knowledge of animals as her father managed a small group of horses and cattle owned by Crassus. It was Crassus who noticed her, during one of his visits to see his animal herds. He suggested she could

---

[6] Meretrix = escort lady , companion

earn a good income elsewhere. Her father could not complain, neither her mother.

Metella felt his sweaty palms wrap around her waist and then the foul smell of Theodore's breath as he attempted to molest her. The small dagger, which she always kept strapped to her right thigh, came into her hand and then it was plunged deep into the neck of the unfortunate discens. She felt in that moment that she had no choice to act as the journey would take 2 more days and she was certain that she would be raped by this lout. She left the broken body of the man where it lay and continued on her way, having taken any coin from him.

Her fears for the horse were founded, when it collapsed on the second day. Fortunately, an Inn was nearby and the Innkeeper was able to provide rough instructions for Deva. Her thoughts for Crassus kept her focussed and as she neared the gates of the port, her heart pounded in anticipation.

She was truly shattered and despondent when she was told that Crassus had been recalled to Rome. Her favourite, private room, had been kept clean in anticipation of her return. Her main source of income had departed and Metella spent many hours in the brothel, weeping with depression.

With all her grieving, she had forgotten about the bracelet. She had put it inside a drawer of the small bedside cabinet and was just opening it when there was a huge explosion.

The brothel, as with many other buildings erected inside the city walls, included a large cellar or basement beneath the ground floor. When Deva was selected as the main outpost in the north, a decision was made to erect a substantial wall to protect the city and it's inhabitants. The wall had 3 main entrances, gated with draw bridges over a moat. The military commanders decided to construct 3 secret escape routes. Deep tunnels to each gate supported with wooden beams. Over the years, the plans of these tunnels had been mislaid and builders were persuaded not to include cellars or basements on any new construction for obvious reasons.the group who built the brothel ignored this advice and included a cellar to store the huge stocks of wines.

It took only a few minutes for the 2 storey brothel to collapse into the void. Unfortunately, Matella and several of her companions perished and were buried along with all the contents of the building.

2005 AD

Chester City council approved the motion to carry out much needed repairs to to the roads in the city centre. The area needing urgent attention was close to the Grosvenor Hotel. Pedestrians and drivers had complained about the pot holes for many years. As soon as repairs were undertaken, more appeared in this area and an in-depth investigation was required. Surveyors believed that the problem lay many metres below the surface. A huge excavator was brought in and began to dig in the area where the surveyor identified the potential problem. Within minutes it became obvious that there was a mass of loose rubble and this would need to be removed prior to refilling with compacted materials. It was the sixth grab of the huge bucket which scooped up, amongst many pieces of rotted wood, a golden charm. Being heavier than the other rubbish, it was flung further into the air. The bracelet landed on a pavement near the Grosvenor Hotel, seconds before a couple strolled in that very place.

FIFTEENTH CHAIN LINK
IN CLIVUM HABITARE. PERICULOSUM

— ◇◇◇ —

Living on a slope is dangerous

2019

Chang had worked and lived in Indonesia for more than 4 years. His parents lived in Malaysia, however he had moved to Indonesia believing that the only real opportunities for lucrative work lie there. During the palm nut gathering period in Malaysia, there was negative unemployment; more jobs than people. This was very seasonal however. He had been very frugal during his years away and was saving for his triumphant return one day and surprise his family. His "find" persuaded him that the time had come for his return to KL. his dream was now a reality.

His sweetheart, the girl he had known since he was just 10 years old, was waiting patiently for him. Hui now worked as a waitress in a very popular restaurant, they had kept in touch and both promised to re-new their friendship when Chang returned. The attractive lady was well liked by the proprietor and the regular customers and had been rewarded with promotion. She was elevated to assistant manager of the Satay Restaurant and it wasn't difficult for her to secure a job for Chang in the kitchens. With his savings and now regular income secured. Chang persuaded Hui that they should move from their very basic accommodation into an apartment in the new development being completed on the outskirts of the city. As planned, on the first day of moving in, Chang produced the bracelet and put it on his girlfriend's wrist. She was overcome with emotion. Her eyes lit up and her skin shone. Her whole appearance improved. Chang somehow knew this would seal his relationship and bring Hui even closer to him.

The next morning, the couple slept in. The previous day had been so eventful. Their new home was in a multi story complex erected on steep sloping ground, north of the city. They were quite pleased that they did not have so many belongings and only the essential pieces of furniture. The builders and owners of this complex had acquired the land in strong competition as Land was at a premium in KL. They felt they had paid far too much for this stretch of land and subsequently found that building on the slopes was a real challenge.

Chang and Hui were about one hour behind schedule and Hui, in particular, began to fret a little about being late. Chang sorted the problem. He would explain to the restaurant owner that Hui was exhausted at just moving in and that he would work the next 12 hours without pay, to make up for her absence. He told Hui to relax, spend a few hours sorting her things and said he would bring a nice meal for both on his return that evening.

At approximately 5 pm, the heavy monsoon rains struck KL. These horrendous storms could become violent and were quite common in this part of Malaysia. On this occasion, the rain became extremely heavy and was probably the most severe for many many years. All traffic stopped and the huge roadside drains could not cope and became fast moving rivers, carrying all before them.

Whilst the builders felt that all regulations had been met when erecting the new apartment blocks, they failed to forecast and calculate the adverse effect of clearing the area of all forestation. Over the centuries, the heavily wooded area could absorb much of the monsoon rains. Large land drains had been built to assist in water drainage and the system had been checked and passed as adequate by the authorities.

This rainfall however was unlike any other and it became obvious that something was amiss when the roadways at the base of the apartments began to overflow, as with the roads in the city.

At 8.00 pm there was a sound, never heard before or since. It sounded and felt like an earthquake with three massive explosions. Three large concrete constructions tumbled down a steep incline. It was caused by the largest mud slide ever witnessed in that part of the world.

Hui had taken a nap shortly after Chang left for work. She was just leaving her flat when the terror struck. Her body, together with another 200, was buried beneath hundreds of tons of concrete, glass and furniture inside the huge mud slurry. Immediately upon learning of the disaster, a young man, working in a restaurant, collapsed. Realising that Hui was gone for ever, and blaming himself for her death, he had a fatal heart attack, brought on by his torment.

2019

Volunteers from around the world offered to help and assist in finding any survivors and clear the rubble. Malaysian authorities were overwhelmed with the kindness as donations from countries and charities poured in. The level of assistance also proved extremely helpful. It was a major task as the rains continued, not as severe, but still enough to cause minor mud slides. It was therefore extremely dangerous and only those with similar experience were invited to partake in the rescue attempt. One of those who qualified and worked so diligently, was Edmund. He was allocated control of a specific area and due to his expertise in prior workings in mud slides, he had a team of 12 others under his control. In such operations, a great deal of trust was required and the honesty of all involved was absolutely paramount. Many valuables were buried and special containers were issued and allocated to each volunteer. The amount of money and jewellery could be substantial and this disaster proved very typical.

After only a few hours of searching, Edmund's character was tested more than at any time in his life. As he lifted a stone figurine, he saw the gleam. The bracelet had been uncovered. It had become detached from Hui's wrist as the first piece of broken structure hit her body. The charm was now safely secured in Edmund's inside pocket. He felt that his container was filling quite adequately and no-one had seen his slight of hand. This was a little reward for the previous 6 years of working in these environments. His devotion to helping others had taken it's toll. He reflected how, 12 months earlier, he had contacted Dangy fever and, nearing death, a special serum was ushered at haste from Singapore to save him. Finding this piece was just deserts, he thought. It was as if the charm was changing his character, for the worse.

Prior to embarking on his volunteer and charity workings, Edmund had been a celebrity. He became so popular in his career of presenting reality shows that he was in constant demand and seemed to have no private life at all. That became unbearable when the media discovered that he had dated the daughter of the most powerful man on the planet. He did not appreciate that every phone call and text, and every meeting would be made public.

The main negative impact was on Savana and, to some extent, her family. This lothario, was well known in the glitz and glam circles, but not to Savana. She was now number 1 target for all the paparazzi. The stories that ensued gripped the whole of the USA, where not much else was happening at the time.

Edmund was banished, never to return and it was this that made him reject his previous way of life and turn to overseas voluntary work. This did not prevent him, years later and realising the harm that he had done, sending a special gift to the only real love of his life.

Savana dedicated her life to "righting the wrongs" as she put it. She became a political animal and very influential in her father's overseas affairs. Her level of tolerance became extremely low, even giving her father some concerns. She would bombast at the slightest peccadillo and become rather asocial. Frequently, she would sit and gaze at her bracelet, however, she had been misled and had no desire to meet up with that low-life again.

Savana became rather sybaritic, probably due to the influence of the wonderful charm, forever gleaming on her wrist. Edmund would get some solace in regularly seeing her on the news channels, wearing and admiring his gift, hoping upon hope that one day they would be together again. Because of her strong and determined character, she formed alliances with many of the world leaders, who respected her views. All leaders, except one in the Far East, who viewed her as inimical; the feeling was mutual.

Savana would assist in creating false news regarding the leader of this communist state and her influence with the media was substantial.

The spurious and evil stories she continued to create eventually became intolerable when the attacks became personal. Her father took a back seat in these matters as it suited his image. He held the power but wanted his opponent in the Far East to deal with his daughter. This caused further anger.

SIXTEENTH THE FAULTY CLASP

FINIS ULTIMO PERFECTUS SINE ANIMI CONSCIENTIA ACCIDIT SED MAGNO CUM DETRIMENTO

◆◆◆

The final end is completed quickly and without conscience. But with great prejudice.

2020

The morning of 4th July was bright and clear. The previous 33 days had been very eventful. Lee Huan had not collapsed and was still treated as a hero in his country, in spite of the serious sanctions which adversely affected the whole population. Instead, he continued to boost his strike capability with the introduction and successful testing of ballistic missiles which could reach the American heartlands. In fact one exchange at the end of June saw an outright threat of first strike if the USA and her in particular did not back down from the continued aggression. This threat was seen as real and the US military advisors suggested a period of calm and caution.

Not so Savana, she felt that this was her domain and persuaded those in command that it warranted a tempered strike, perhaps non nuclear, at several of their air bases, near the coast and away from population. "Verbal warnings were not effective and sanctions useless against this tyrant," she expleated.

She had the ear of the Commander in Chief, so later that beautiful morning, on that famous date, several US aircraft took off from the carrier and headed for the nearest coastal base. The enemy was prepared and downed all 3 aircraft, with no survivors.

To coincide with this attack, and history has a habit of dealing the cards this way, Lee Huan had decided to have a test run of 2 of his new missiles. Not armed, but to test distance and accuracy. In theory his scientists gave assurances they could reach the USA, however, he felt that proving the capability would boost his powers of negotiation with the irritating female. The engineers controlling these 2 launches would destroy the missiles within 60 seconds of take off, having sufficient calculations to firm up that requirements had been met.

The US missile defence and warning system had not been updated for some time and essentially, needed a complete overhaul, as engineers' reports verified. Some knowledgeable Defence personnel were rather worried that there might be a repeat of the famous incident in September 1983. This event showed, on the Russian defence system, that the US had launched 5 nuclear missiles aimed at Russian targets. Under extreme pressure from his engineers and command, the colonel in charge of the retaliation system, refused to launch a counter attack. Stanislav Petrov is the man who saved the world, as, if he had given the permission to launch, then a full blown nuclear war and ultimate destruction of our planet would have ensued. As it happened, he was suspicious that US would only launch 5 missiles and he was able to determine the correct decision. In the analysis that followed, the Russian missile defence system had proven faulty and rectified very quickly. The main point to make is that the Colonel was able to determine in his thinking, under extreme pressure, the correct logic. He was not commended for his actions and neither the world appreciated this man's immense intelligence in those moments.

Savana was completely oblivious to any such matters and when she learned of the failure of the air strike and simultaneous launch of 2 ballistic missiles, her mind became uncontrollable. She persuaded her father to take that decision which would ultimately destroy the planet. The launches took place at 10 pm US time and within 48 hours, the earth and all within it, including the charm, was reduced to powder. The planet was returned to the time, pre Dinosaur

FINITO

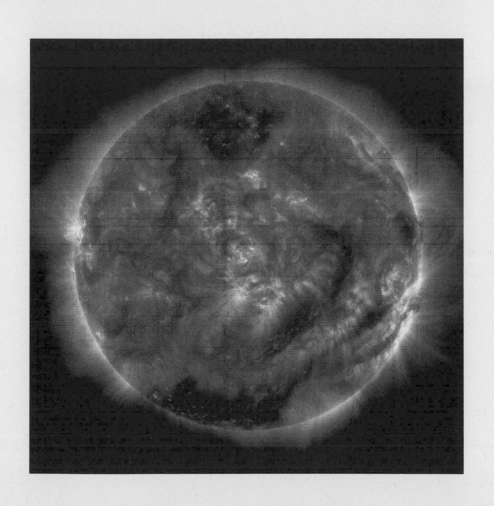

ABOUT THE AUTHOR

Alan worked in Sales for a world leader in supply of safety and survival equipment. During his 35 years in post, he travelled to 23 countries and visited more than 80 cities.He retired in 2005 and the book was inspired by some of the experiences and tales during his travels.

He now enjoys spending time with his family members especially his brothers. Children and grandchildren. He is presently struggling to learn Italian and the piano.

Printed and bound by PG in the USA